My dinosaur is more awesome!

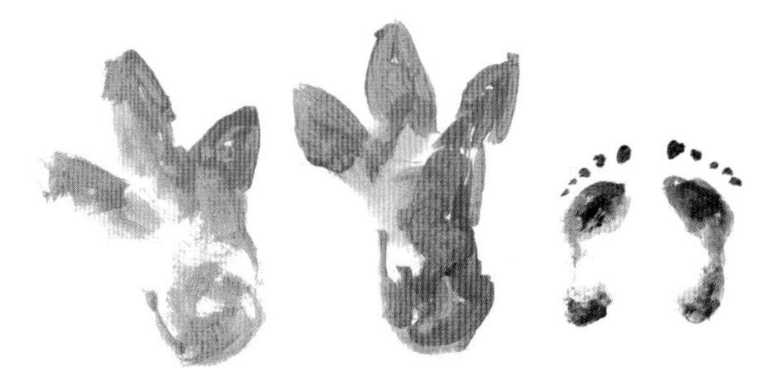

For Vikki, Will, Phoebe, and Louis,
and, of course, Joel and Olivia!

Layout and design by Pixooma

Sky Pony Press books may be purchased in bulk at special discounts for sales promotion, corporate gifts, fund-raising, or educational purposes. Special editions can also be created to specifications. For details, contact the Special Sales Department, Sky Pony Press, 307 West 36th Street, 11th Floor, New York, NY 10018 or info@skyhorsepublishing.com.

Visit our website at www.skyponypress.com.

10 9 8 7 6 5 4 3 2 1

Manufactured in China, November 2014
This product conforms to CPSIA 2008
Library of Congress Cataloging-in-Publication Data is available on file.

Print ISBN: 978-1-63220-416-5
Ebook ISBN: 978-1-63220-831-6

Story and illustrations by Simon Coster

Sky Pony Press
New York

This
awesome
book
belongs
to
Your name:

JOEL and OLIVIA sat down for dinner

of homemade soup and bread

with two of their FAVORITE DINOSAURS,

when Olivia pointed and said . . .

"My dinosaur is better than YOURS.
Her clothes are always in style.
She has a closet just for shoes and hats
and a bag made of NILE CROCODILE!"

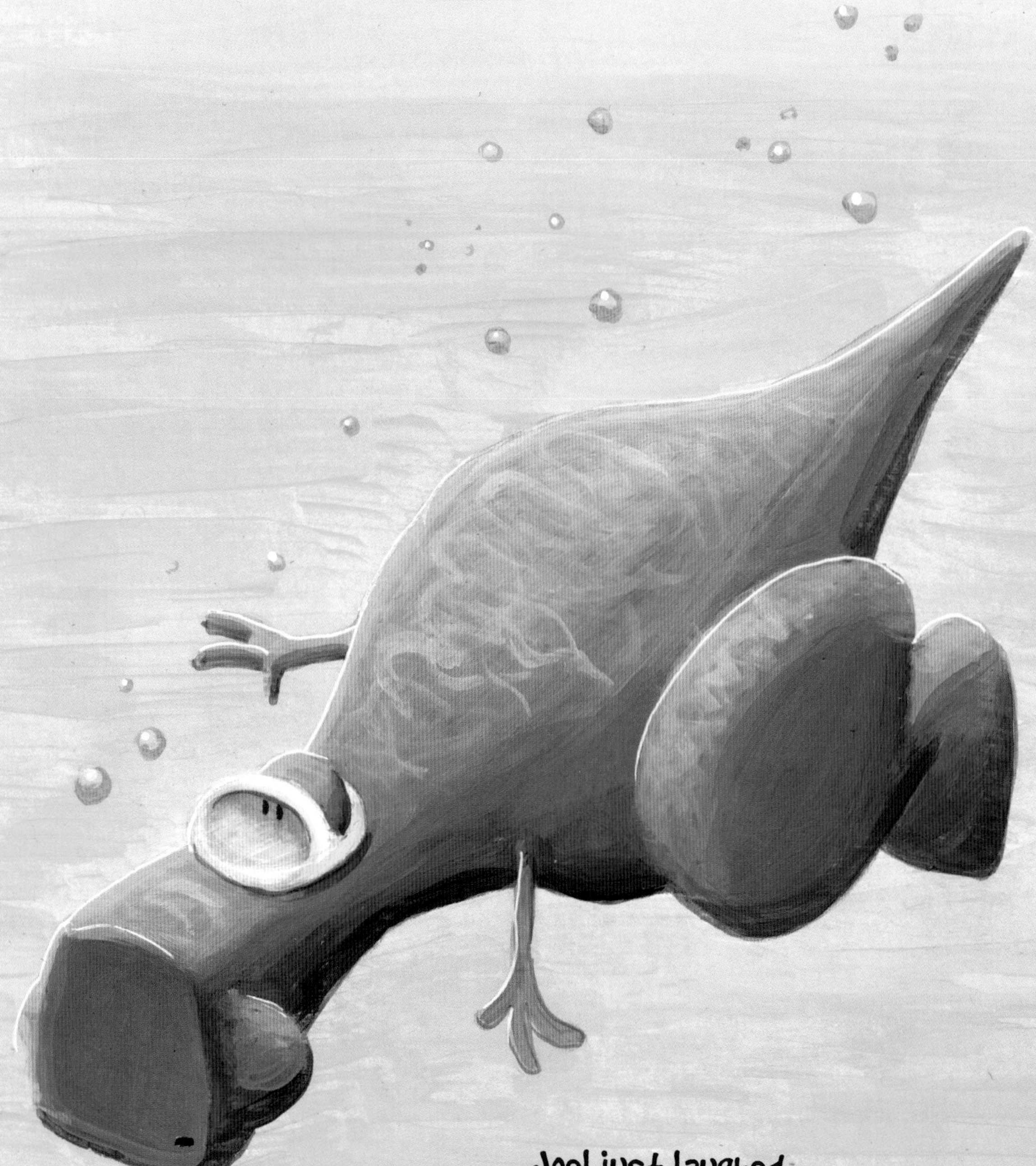

Joel just laughed.

“That's NOTHING! My dinosaur can swim like a shark.

He stays up till quarter past seven,

and his teeth sometimes **GLOW** in the dark!

jumping
“He's really good at jumping

and sliding on his knees.

"He even has X-ray vision,

and he's not afraid of bees!"

Olivia shrugged, then glared at Joel.

"MY DINOSAUR makes her own jam.

She EATS electric eels

AND drives an ice cream van!

“She’s best
at walking
backwards;

keeps a unicorn
in the attic.

"She can play the trumpet
while riding her bike,

and her house is the shape of a rabbit!"

“MY DINOSAUR
wrestles
horses.

He can also
run through
METAL.

“He’s awesome at
hide-and-go-seek

and can hold a
stinging nettle!"

"My dinosaur can eat a WHOLE cactus!"
"My dinosaur eats five in his SLEEP!"
Z Z Z Z Z

"My dinosaur once made her own sweater . . .

. . . with the wool still attached to the SHEEP!"

“My dinosaur can stand on one leg for TWO MINUTES, then swap and stand on the other.

He can play the
guitar WITHOUT
using his hands,

and he has an
INVISIBLE brother!"

"That's quite enough!" said Mommy.

"All I've heard is you argue and moan.

You're not the ONLY two people

to have a dinosaur of their OWN!"

“MY DINOSAUR
eats lions for
breakfast

and enjoys a delicious
ELEPHANT roast.

"He once ate a
WHOLE VOLCANO,

although this morning
he just ate toast!

“ His bike is encrusted
with DIAMONDS.

He can also travel through TIME.

“His slippers are
the color of
rainbows,

“and his toots smell
of lemon and lime!

TRUUUMP!

"Now, you both have fantastic dinosaurs,

but there can be only one winner.

It's my dinosaur that is BEST OF ALL,

so go on and eat your dinner."